Tonka
BIG CITY DUMP TRUCK

Written by Mary Packard
Illustrated by Thomas LaPadula

SCHOLASTIC INC.
New York Toronto London Auckland Sydney

Look for these other books about Tonka trucks:
Working Hard with the Busy Fire Truck
Working Hard with the Mighty Dump Truck
Working Hard with the Mighty Loader
Working Hard with the Mighty Mixer
Building the New School
Fire Truck to the Rescue
Working Hard with the Mighty Tractor Trailer and Bulldozer
Working Hard with the Rescue Helicopter
Big Farm Tractor

ISBN 0-590-05656-5

10 9 8 7 6 5 4 3 2 1

Printed in the U.S.A. 24

First printing, May 1997

HONNNNNNNK! HONNNNNNK!
Whoa! thought Chris. *That sure is a loud horn.*
Chris raced to the window to see what kind of truck
could have made such a sound. *One thing's for sure,*
he thought. *It's a big one!*

Sure enough, an enormous dump truck was
coming right down his block.
"Mom!" shouted Chris. "Come quick!"
Chris's mother joined him at the window. They
had a good view. That is because they lived on the
eleventh floor of a very tall skyscraper.

The dump truck parked beside the empty lot
next door.
The driver got out to hang a sign on the fence.
"'Construction Site,'" read Chris's mother.
"See the picture of the skyscraper?" asked Chris.
"I sure do," replied his mother. "That's what they
are going to build," she added.
"Cool!" cried Chris.

"I wish I could see the dump truck up close," said Chris.
"Perhaps we can," said Chris's mother. "Let's go ask the driver."
Chris and his mother rode the elevator down to the first floor. They
hurried outside to the construction site.

Chris waved to the driver.
"Hi, my name is Chris and this is my mother," he said.
"Glad to meet you both," said the driver. "My name is Dave."
Dave stood beside his bright yellow dump truck. It was huge, with tires that were taller than Chris.
"Would you like to climb aboard?" he asked.
Chris's eyes sparkled. "Yes!" he said.

Dave reached up and opened the door to the cab.
Then he lifted Chris onto the running board.
Chris scrambled into the seat, and Dave sat down beside him.

"This is where all the controls are," he said. "The steering wheel, the brakes, the gas pedal, and the gearshift."
He even let Chris try out the horn. *HONNNNNNK!*

Dave started up the engine. The mighty
truck rumbled.
"Look through the back window," he said
to Chris.
Dave pulled on a lever.
Suddenly the front of the truck bed tilted up,
up, up until it was way up in the sky.

Dave pulled on the lever again.
Now the truck bed went down, down, down
until it fit back into place with a *CLANG!*
"That's all for now," said Dave as he
helped Chris out of the truck. "Time
to get back to work. I have to clear
the site."

"Thank you for showing us
your dump truck," said Chris.
"My pleasure," said Dave.

Dave set out cones in the street to keep traffic away.
Soon a very big truck pulled up between the cones. It
was a long-bed trailer with a power excavator on top.
Dave unlocked the gate and helped guide the trailer
into the construction site.

The power excavator had long treads wrapped around
its wheels. (The treads made it easy to drive over rough
ground.) Chris watched the excavator slowly back off
the trailer.

He saw the driver move some levers in the cab. Suddenly
the shovel moved up and down on its folding arm.

"It looks like a dinosaur," said Chris.

The trailer drove away.
Dave backed the dump truck through the open gate
and parked it in front of the excavator.
The excavator scooped up its first load.
It lifted it high and dumped it into the back of Dave's truck.

BOOM! The dump truck shuddered as
the heavy load of dirt landed with a thud.

Pretty soon the truck was almost full. "Where will all that dirt get dumped?" asked Chris.

"Let's find out," said Chris's mother. They walked across the street to the parking garage to get their car.

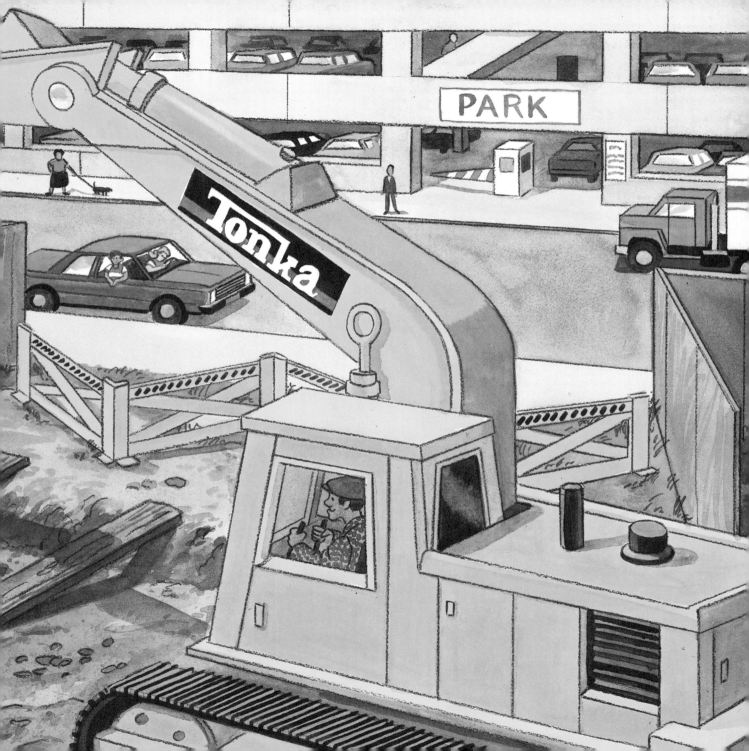

When the dump truck was full, Dave drove through the gate.
"Here we go," said Chris's mother.
They followed Dave and his mighty dump truck through the city streets.
When they got to the corner, a police officer stopped the traffic
so the big truck could make a wide turn.

They followed the truck to the river.
BEEP, BEEP, BEEP went the truck as it backed up to the loading dock. There was a huge barge waiting.

Dave pulled the lever, and the truck bed rose up, up, up. Then with a loud *CRASH!* the truck dropped its full load right onto the barge.

"Nice aim!" exclaimed Chris.

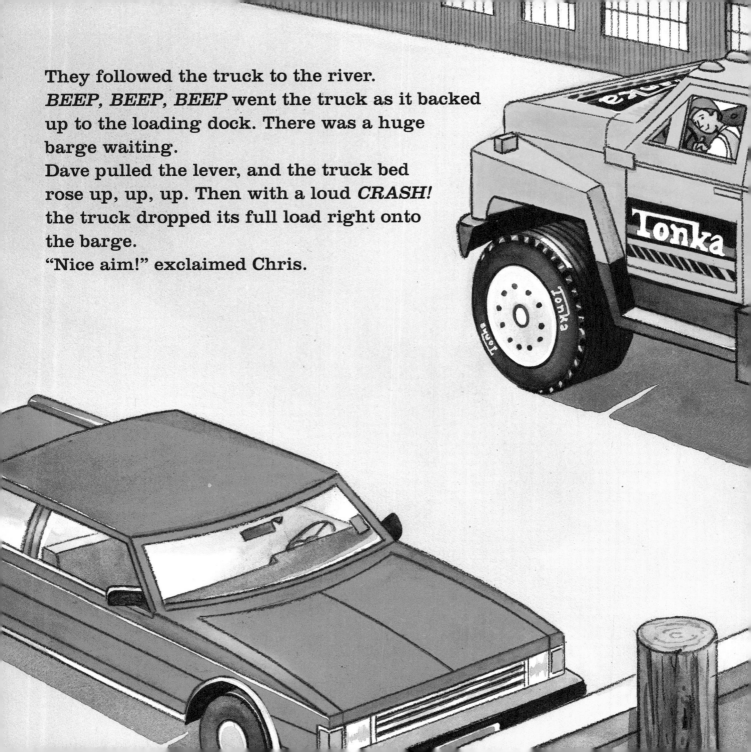

Chris and his mother stopped to buy coffee
and doughnuts for the construction workers.
When they got back, Chris helped his mother hand out the treats.

"Thank you," said Dave, and he introduced Chris and his mother to his friends. "Wait until you see all the trucks that will be here next week."

"What kinds of trucks?" asked Chris.
"Oh, let's see now," said Dave. "A cement mixer,
a grader, a crane . . . "
Chris's face lit up with excitement.
He could hardly wait to see them — as long as his
favorite dump truck came back, too.